W9-CIJ-224

DATE DUE

SE 22 '00			
NO 3 '00			
OCT 3 0 2003			
OCT 2 1 2005			
OCT 1 2 2007			
OCT 1 4 2014			

Three Stories
You Can Read
to Your Cat

Sara Swan Miller

Illustrated by True Kelley

Houghton Mifflin Company
Boston

For Pippin and Merry's best friends,
Chris and Erin
—S.S.M.

For the Pumpkin Hill kitties:
Willa, Natty, Alice, Vinny, and Woody
—T.K.

Text copyright © 1997 by Sara Swan Miller
Illustrations copyright © 1997 by True Kelley

The text of this book is set in 16-pt. Baskerville.
The illustrations are ink and watercolor.

Library of Congress Cataloging-in-Publication Data

Miller, Sara Swan.
    Three stories you can read to your cat / Sara Swan Miller ;
illustrated by True Kelley.
    p.   cm.
    Summary: A cat hears three stories about a dull rainy day,
a yummy bug, and a good day of destruction in the house.
    RNF ISBN 0-395-78831-5   PAP ISBN 0-395-95752-4
    [Cats—Fiction.]   I. Kelley, True, ill.   II. Title
PZ7.M63344Tg   1996   96-51
[E]—dc20   CIP
                            AC

Printed in Singapore
TWP 10 9 8 7 6 5 4 3

Contents

Introduction

Does your cat sleep a lot? Most cats do. Why do cats sleep so much? Maybe they cannot think of anything else to do. Maybe they get bored. What if you had to sit inside all day? You might get bored, too.

What do you do when you are bored? You can always read a good book. But cats cannot read.

You can do a nice thing for your cat. You can read these stories out loud. Your cat will like them. They are about things cats understand best.

Invite your cat to come hear a story. Ask nicely. Cats hate being told what to do.

Be sure to pet your cat while you read. Cats like petting almost as much as stories.

Here, Kitty Kitty. Would you like to sit on my lap? Would you like to hear a story? This one is just for you.

1

The Rainy Day

ONE DAY you woke up early.
You were ready for fun!
You jumped up on the windowsill.
"PHOOEY!" you said. "It is raining!
This is no good!"
The rain did not stop. There was nothing
to do.

You curled up on the couch. And you went
back to sleep.

After a while, you woke up.
It was still raining!
"This is terrible!" you said.
"What am I going to do all day?"

You sat down and
gave yourself a bath.

You licked and licked and licked.
You cleaned your ears.

You cleaned your tail.

You even cleaned
between your toes.

Finally, there was nothing more to clean.
You jumped back on the windowsill.

"Rats!" you said.
"It is STILL RAINING!"

You jumped back down.

You went to sit under the dining table. "Maybe some food will fall," you said to yourself. "Sometimes food does that."

But nothing fell. And nothing fell. So you gave up. You jumped back on the windowsill.

IT WAS STILL RAINING!

"I have had enough of this rain!" you said.

"I will *make* it stop raining!"

You crouched on the sill. You closed your eyes up tight. You sent loud thoughts at the rain.

"Stop, rain!" you thought very loudly.

STOP, RAIN! STOP, RAIN!
STOP, RAIN! STOP, RAIN!
STOP, RAIN!

You did it a hundred times.

At last, you opened your eyes.
The rain had stopped!
"I am an amazing cat!" you said to yourself.

You ran to the door.

"OUT! OUT! NOW!" you called.
"NOW! NOW! NOW! NOW!
NOWWWWWWW!
NOWWWWWWW!"

"Oh," said your friend. "Do you want to
go out?"
"What a stupid question," you said to yourself.
The door opened.
"Look!" said your friend. "The rain has
stopped!"

"I know," you said. And you walked out
into the sunshine.

Hey there, you nice kitty.
Would you like more stories?
Here is another one for you.

2

The Yummy Bug

ONE DAY you were sleeping in a patch of
sun on the kitchen floor. The floor was nice
and cool. The sun was good and warm.
It was a fine place for a nap.

You heard a tiny noise. "Tic tic tic tic tic."
You opened your eyes.
A little bug was running across the floor.
"Ah!" you said to yourself. "A yummy bug!"
"Come here, yummy bug," you called.
"I want to eat you."

The bug ran and hid
in a crack.
"I see you, yummy
bug," you said.
"Come out, now!"

But the yummy bug did not come out.
"I don't care, yummy bug," you said.
"I can wait."
You sat still. You didn't move even a whisker.
You waited.

The bug stuck its head out of the crack.

It crawled slowly out. It came crawling across the floor.
You sat very still. The yummy bug crawled closer.

Your tail gave a twitch! The bug ran behind a chair.

"Hmmf!" you said to yourself.

"I see you, yummy bug," you called.

The bug hid behind a chair leg.

"I don't care, yummy bug," you said.

"I can wait." You sat very, very still.

You waited and waited.

The bug poked its
nose around
the chair leg.

It wiggled its feelers. Then it crept out from
behind the chair. It came creeping across
the floor.

You sat still. The yummy bug crept closer.
"Don't twitch, tail," you said. The bug crept
even closer.

Your left ear gave a flick! The yummy bug
ran behind the garbage can.
"Phooey!" you said to yourself.

"I can still see you, bug," you called.
The bug hid under the garbage can.
"I don't care, yummy bug," you said.
"I can wait. I can wait forever."
You sat very, very, very still. You waited
and waited and waited.

Finally, the bug stuck out its feelers.

Then it stuck out its head.

You sat stiller than still.

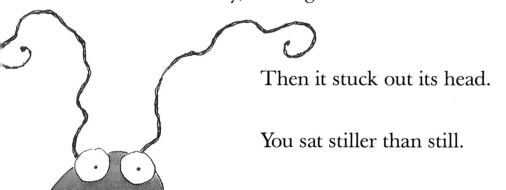

The yummy bug sneaked out from under
the garbage can. It tiptoed across the floor.
You sat still as a stone. The yummy bug
tiptoed closer.

"Don't twitch, tail," you said.
"Don't flick, ear."

The yummy bug
tiptoed closer.

And closer.

It tiptoed right under your nose.
"Thank you, yummy bug," you said.

You lapped it right up.

The bug tasted AWFUL!

"Poo!" you said. "Ick!"
You spat it out. The bug ran away
as fast as its tiny legs could take it.

"You nasty bug, you!" you called after it.
"Why did you let me eat you? You know
I hate bugs!"

You licked the bad taste off on your paw.
Then you curled up in the sunshine again,
and you went back to your nap.

Are you still there, Kitty?
You must like stories. Would you
like one more? This is the last one.

3

The Good Day

ONE DAY your friend went to the door.
"I am going out, Kitty," said your friend.
"Now be good. Don't do anything bad while
I am gone."
Your friend went out the door.

"Why would I want to do anything bad?"
you asked yourself. "Bad things are no good."
Your friend was so silly!

You looked around for
something good to do.
A curtain was blowing in
the wind.
"Climbing is always fun,"
you said to yourself. "And
fun is good!"
You stuck out your strong
claws. You began to climb
up the curtain. You climbed
all the way to the top.

Then you jumped
back down.

"That was a very good thing
to do," you said to yourself.
"I think I will do it again."

So you climbed up the curtain again.
Then you climbed it again.

And again.

And again.

"Hm," you said to yourself. "There are too
many holes in this curtain now. But it was
very good while it lasted!"

You looked around for something else good
to do. A green plant was growing on the
windowsill. You jumped up next to it.
"This plant looks good," you said.
You nibbled on a leaf. The plant was VERY
good. You nibbled all the nice green tips.

"Mmmmm," you said to yourself.
"That was very, very good."

A little rug was lying on the floor.
"Cleaning my claws is always a good thing
to do," you said to the rug.
You sunk your claws into the rug.
You worked and worked. You worked until
your claws were good and clean and sharp.

"Ah," you said to yourself. "That was very,
very, very good."

A bowl was sitting on the table. You jumped up next to it. You looked in the bowl. There was something inside! You stuck your paw in the bowl and felt all around.

"What is this Thing in the bowl?" you asked yourself. "It would be good to find out."

You fished around in the bowl.
The Thing would not come out!

You fished around some more.
And some more.

CRASH!

The bowl fell on the floor.

You jumped down and looked at the Thing.
You gave it a poke.

"Oh," you said to the Thing. "You are just a
piece of paper. Oh well. It is good to know,
anyway."

You went looking for more good things to do.
You prowled all around the house.
You prowled here.

You prowled there.

Finally, you prowled your way into the
kitchen. A can was sitting on the floor.
"What is that Good Smell?" you asked
the can. "It would be very, very good
to find out."

You knocked off the lid and looked inside.
You stuck in your paw. Was this the Good
Smell? No. You tossed it on the floor. Was
this the Good Smell? No. Or this? No.
Or this? You dug and dug in the can. You dug
all the way to the bottom.

"Aha!" you said. "Here you are, Smell!"
A wonderful piece of chicken!
"This is better than good," you said.
"This is GREAT!"

You munched and you crunched.
You crunched and you munched.
You munched and crunched up every last bit.

"Mmmmm," you said. "Ahhh! That was the best thing I have done all day!"

Doing all those good things made you very
sleepy. You crept back to the living room.
You jumped up on the couch and curled
yourself into a ball.
"What a good day I had today!" you said
to yourself.

"My friend will be happy. I did not do
one bad thing!"
You wrapped your tail over your nose,
and you went to sleep.

The End